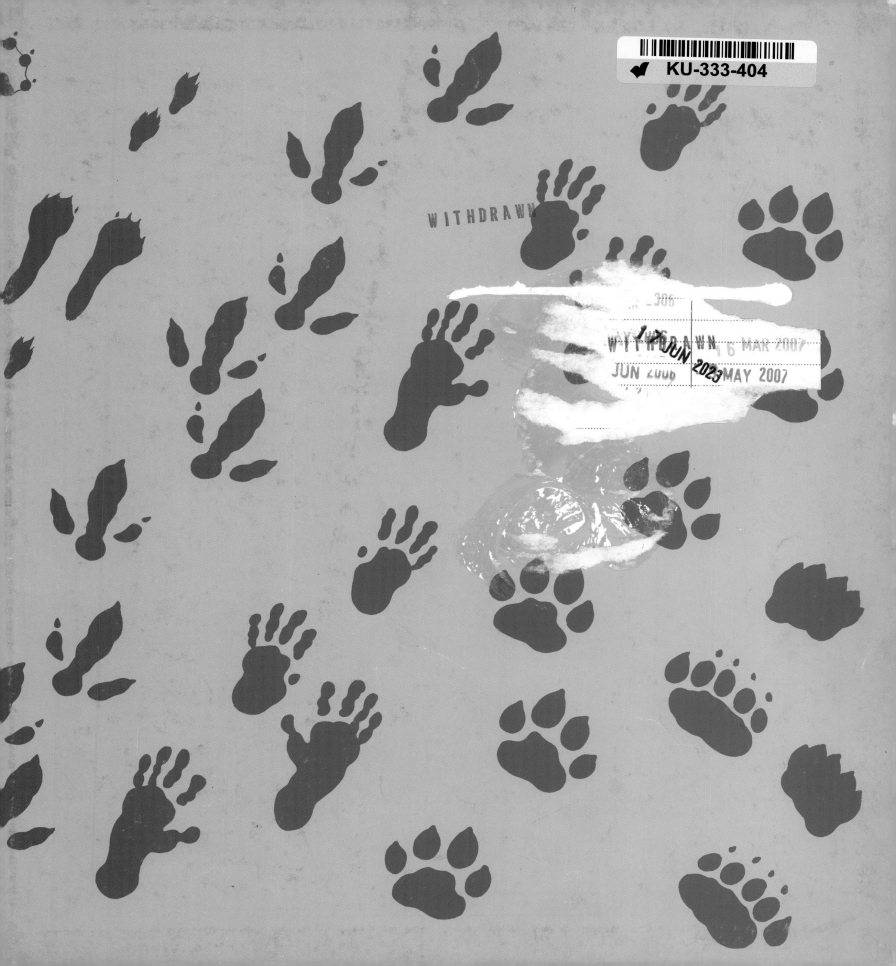

For Jack

343688

ORCHARD BOOKS
96 Leonard Street, London EC2A 4XD
Orchard Books Australia
32-45/51 Huntley Street, Alexandria, NSW 2015
1 84362 186 X
First published in Great Britain in 2003
Text and illustrations © John Butler 2003
The right of John Butler to be identified as the author and illustrator of this work
has been asserted by him in accordance with the Copyright, Designs and Patents Act, 1988.
A CIP catalogue record for his book is available from the British Library.
1 3 5 7 9 10 8 6 4 2
Printed in Singapore

Can You Cuddle Like a Koala?

John Butler

ORCHARD BOOKS

Out in the wild,

what can you be?

Can you copy these creatures?

Are you ready?

Let's see.

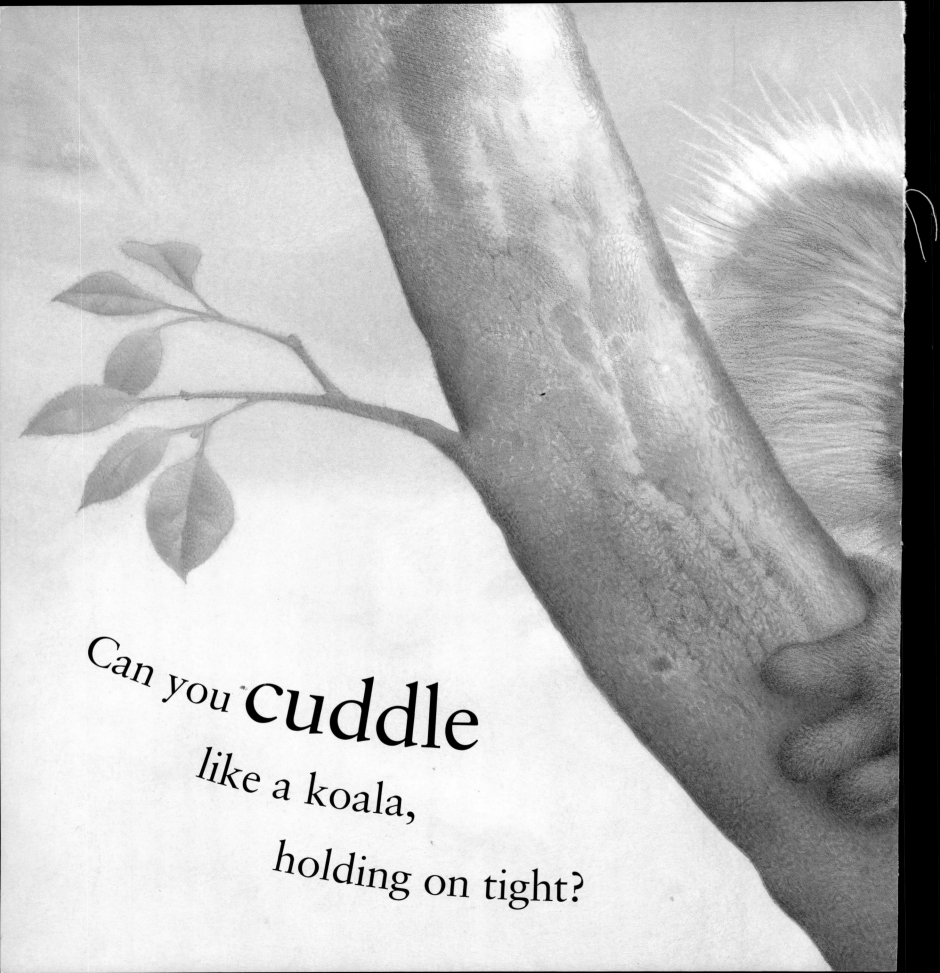

Can you **cuddle**
like a koala,
holding on tight?

Can you **creep** like a mouse

in the pale moonlight?

Can you swing

like a monkey in the tall, swaying trees?

Can you **wink** like an owl, hiding in the leaves?

Can you

leap like a frog
in the bubbling stream?

Can you **stretch**

like a tiger, waking from a dream?

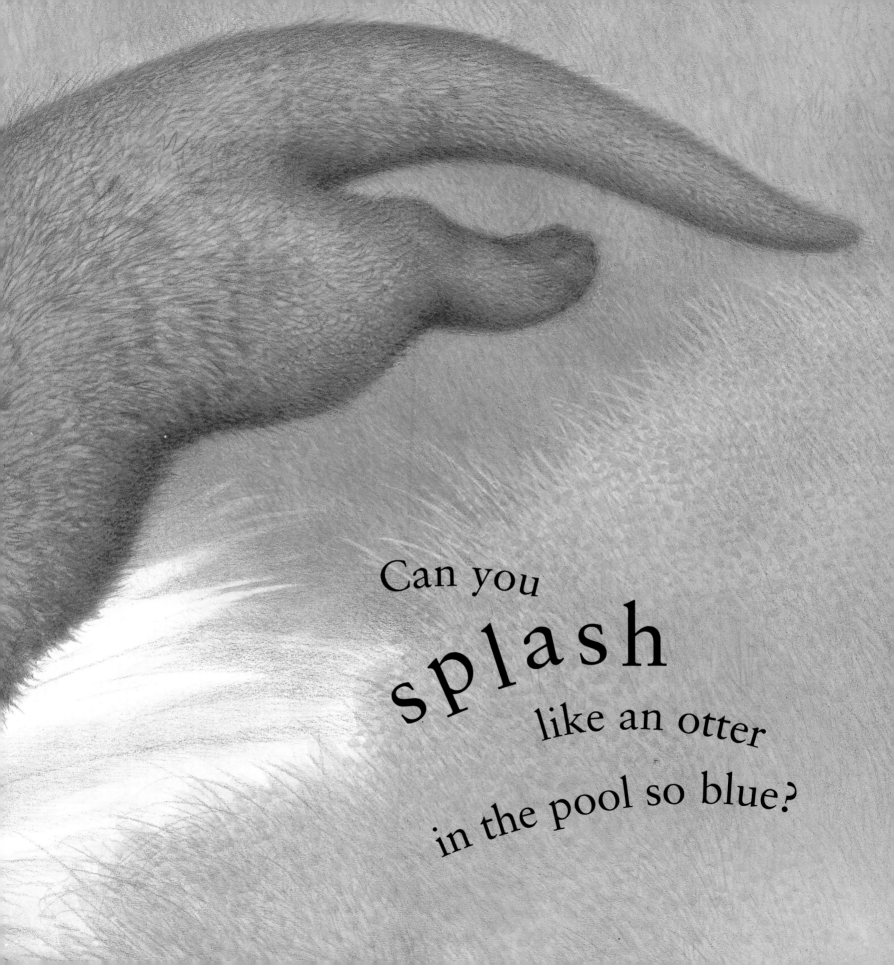

Can you

splash

like an otter

in the pool so blue?

Can you jump like a hare,

chasing through the dew?

Can you hug
like a bear,

with all your might?

Can you curl up like a squirrel getting ready for the night?

Now look at these creatures, all ready for bed.

Can you copy them too,

and rest your head?